Kipper's First Match

Written by Roderick Hunt and Annemarie Young
Illustrated by Alex Brychta

OXFORD

UNIVERSITY PRESS

Sam was excited. Rush Green was through to Round 3 of the FA Cup. It was only a small team, but now it would play against East Ham.

Sam's dad was the captain of Rush Green.
"The match will be on TV," said Sam.

"When we play East Ham," Sam said, "I'll lead the team onto the pitch. I'm the mascot for this game."

"Brilliant!" said Kipper.

When Kipper got home, he was excited. Sam's mum had invited Kipper to go to the big match with them.

"It's not fair," said Chip. "Kipper doesn't even like football."

"Stop it, Chip," said Dad. "Maybe I can take you and Biff to the match."

The next day Dad tried to buy tickets for the match,
but they were sold out. Chip and Biff were disappointed.

When Sam came round to show off his football strip,
Chip went up to his room and slammed the door.

10

Kipper went to the match with Sam's mum and
grandad. A big crowd of people was moving towards
the gate.

Kipper went through a turnstile into the football ground.

"If you need the toilet, you'd better go now," said Sam's mum.

They had special seats next to the tunnel.

"The players come out onto the pitch here," said Sam's grandad.

There were thousands of fans in the stands. All the Rush Green fans were at one end. They all wore green and white.

Hammy, the East Ham club mascot, came onto the pitch. There was a huge roar from the East Ham fans.

"It's so loud," said Kipper.

There was a great cheer from all the fans as the players ran on. Sam was next to his dad. He carried the ball.

The Rush Green team lined up for a photo. Then it was time for the match to begin.

Sam came and sat next to Kipper. "Come on Rush Green!" yelled Sam.

Rush Green had the ball in the East Ham half of the pitch.

A Rush Green player kicked a high cross into the penalty area. Sam's dad headed the ball . . . and scored! The Rush Green fans went wild!

At half-time, Sam's mum went to get hot pies.

"Wow!" said Sam. "Rush Green is leading by one goal in the first half."

"One up!" said Kipper. "Ace!"

Their excitement didn't last. East Ham were in the Rush Green end for most of the second half.

The East Ham players began to look strong. The ball slammed into the crossbar – almost a goal! Ten minutes later, they scored.

Then a Rush Green player fouled an East Ham striker – a penalty to East Ham! They took it and scored.

"Oh no! Two–one," said Sam.

"Two–one. Sorry, Dad," said Sam after the match was over.

"It was good to score," said Sam's dad. "We didn't expect to win."

Sam's dad had a present for Sam and Kipper – footballs signed by all the East Ham players.

"Fantastic," said Kipper.

"This is for you," said Kipper.

"And this is for you," said Chip. "We recorded the match. It was great seeing you on TV."

26

Talk about the story

Why was Sam excited?

Why did Chip slam the door?

How did the match end?

What makes watching a football match so exciting?

The football pitch

Halfway line

Corner flag

Penalty box

Centre circle

Centre spot

Penalty spot

Goal

6 yard box

Goal-line

Touchline

28

Right back

Striker

Central
defender

Midfielders

Goalkeeper

Striker

Central
defender

Left back

Spot the difference

Find the five differences in the two pictures of Sam.

Kipper's First Pet

Learning to Swim

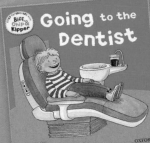
Going to the Dentist

Going to the Hairdresser

Going to the Doctor

Going on a Plane

Let's Recycle!

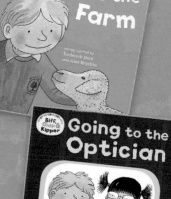
Fun at the Farm

Kipper Gets Nits

Going to the Hospital

Going to the Optician

Starting School

FIRST EXPERIENCES Flashcards
55 cards

Kipper's First Dance Class

A New Baby

Kipper's First Match

Going to the Vet

Series created by Roderick Hunt and Alex Brychta

Read with Biff, Chip and Kipper
The UK's best-selling home reading series

Phonics

First Stories

	Phonics				First Stories			
Level 1 Getting ready to read	Kipper's Alphabet I Spy	Chip's Letter Sounds	Biff's Wonder Words	Floppy's Fun Phonics	Get On	Floppy Did This!	Up You Go	Six in a Bed
Level 2 Starting to read	I am Kipper	Cat in a Bag	The Red Hen	The Fizz-Buzz	Funny Fish	Silly Races!	The Snowman	Dad's Birthday
Level 3 Becoming a reader	Such a Fuss	Shops	The Sing Song	The Backpack	Poor Old Rabbit	I Can Trick a Tiger	Super Dad	Floppy and the Bone
Level 4 Developing as a reader	Wet Feet	The Moon Jet	The Red Coat	Quick! Quick!	Missing!	The Raft Race	Dragon Danger	The Spaceship
Level 5 Building confidence in reading	Egg Fried Rice	Craig Saves the Day	Seasick	Dolphin Rescue	Hungry Floppy	Husky Adventure	Trapped!	Looking after Gran
Level 6 Reading with confidence	Gran's New Blue Shoes	Ice City	Save Pudding Wood	Uncle Max	Hairy-Scary Monster	Mountain Rescue	The Lost Voice	Secret of the Sands

Phonics stories help children practise their sounds and letters, as they learn to do in school.

First Stories have been specially written to provide practice in reading everyday language.

OXFORD
UNIVERSITY PRESS

Great Clarendon Street, Oxford OX2 6DP

Text © Roderick Hunt and Annemarie Young 2009

Illustrations © Alex Brychta 2009

First published 2009

This edition published 2014

10 9 8 7 6 5 4 3 2 1

Series Editors: Kate Ruttle, Annemarie Young

British Library Cataloguing in Publication Data available

ISBN: 978-0-19-273679-6

Printed in China by Imago

The characters in this work are the original creation of Roderick Hunt and Alex Brychta who retain copyright in the characters.